EVERYBODY IN THE RED BRICK BUILDING

written by **ANNE WYNTER**   illustrated by **OGE MORA**

BALZER + BRAY
An Imprint of HarperCollinsPublishers

Balzer + Bray is an imprint of HarperCollins Publishers.

Everybody in the Red Brick Building
Text copyright © 2021 by Anne Wynter
Illustrations copyright © 2021 by Oge Mora
All rights reserved. Manufactured in Italy.

Library of Congress Control Number: 2019040566
ISBN 978-0-06-286576-2

The artist used acrylic paint, gouache, china markers, patterned paper, pastels,
and old book clippings to create the collage illustrations for this book.
Typography by Dana Fritts
21 22 23 24 25 RTLO 10 9 8 7 6 5 4 3 2 1

First Edition

For my parents.
Thank you for all the books.
-A.W.

To Baby Chiji
-O.M.

Everybody in the red brick building was asleep.

Until . . .

Baby Izzie sat up in her crib and howled.

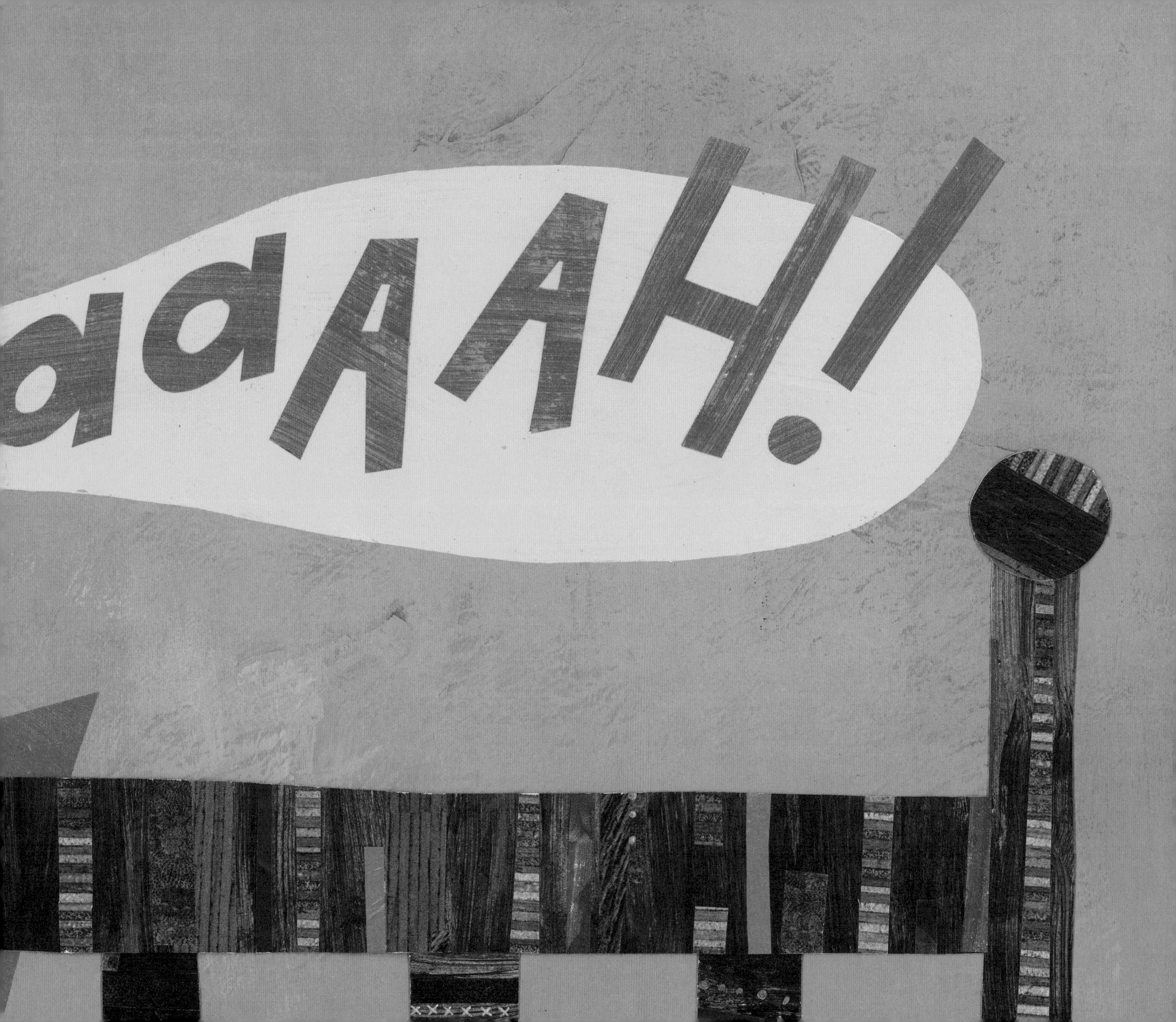
aaAAH!

Woken up by a **WaaaAAH!**,
Rayhan tiptoed out of bed
to check on his parrot.

Rraak!
WAKE UP!

Woken up by a **WaaaAAH!**
and a **Rraak! Wake up!**,
Benny pulled Cairo and Miles
from their sleeping bags
and challenged them to a game
of flashlight tag.

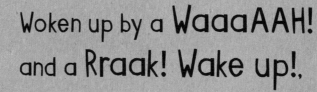

Pitter
patter
STOMP!

Woken up by a WaaaAAH!,
a Rraak! Wake up!,
and a Pitter patter STOMP!,
Natalia dropped from her bunk to
launch her brand-new light-up rocket.

PSSSHEEEW!

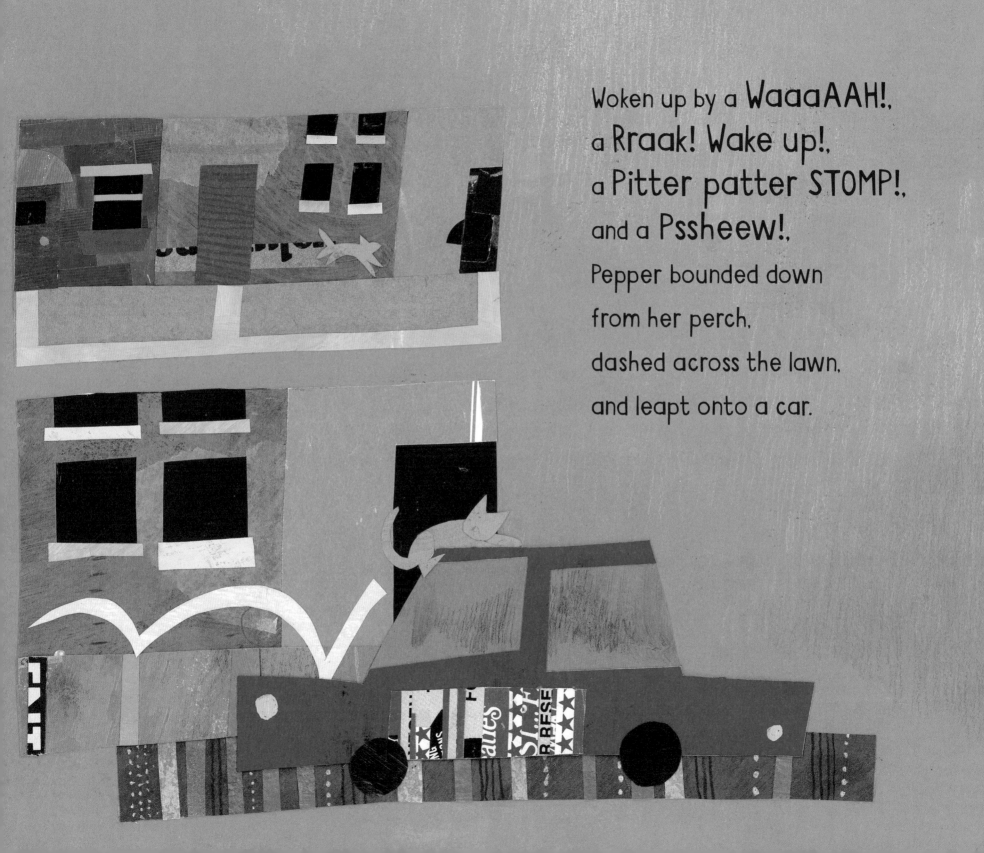

Woken up by a WaaaAAH!,
a Rraak! Wake up!,
a Pitter patter STOMP!,
and a Pssheew!,
Pepper bounded down
from her perch,
dashed across the lawn,
and leapt onto a car.

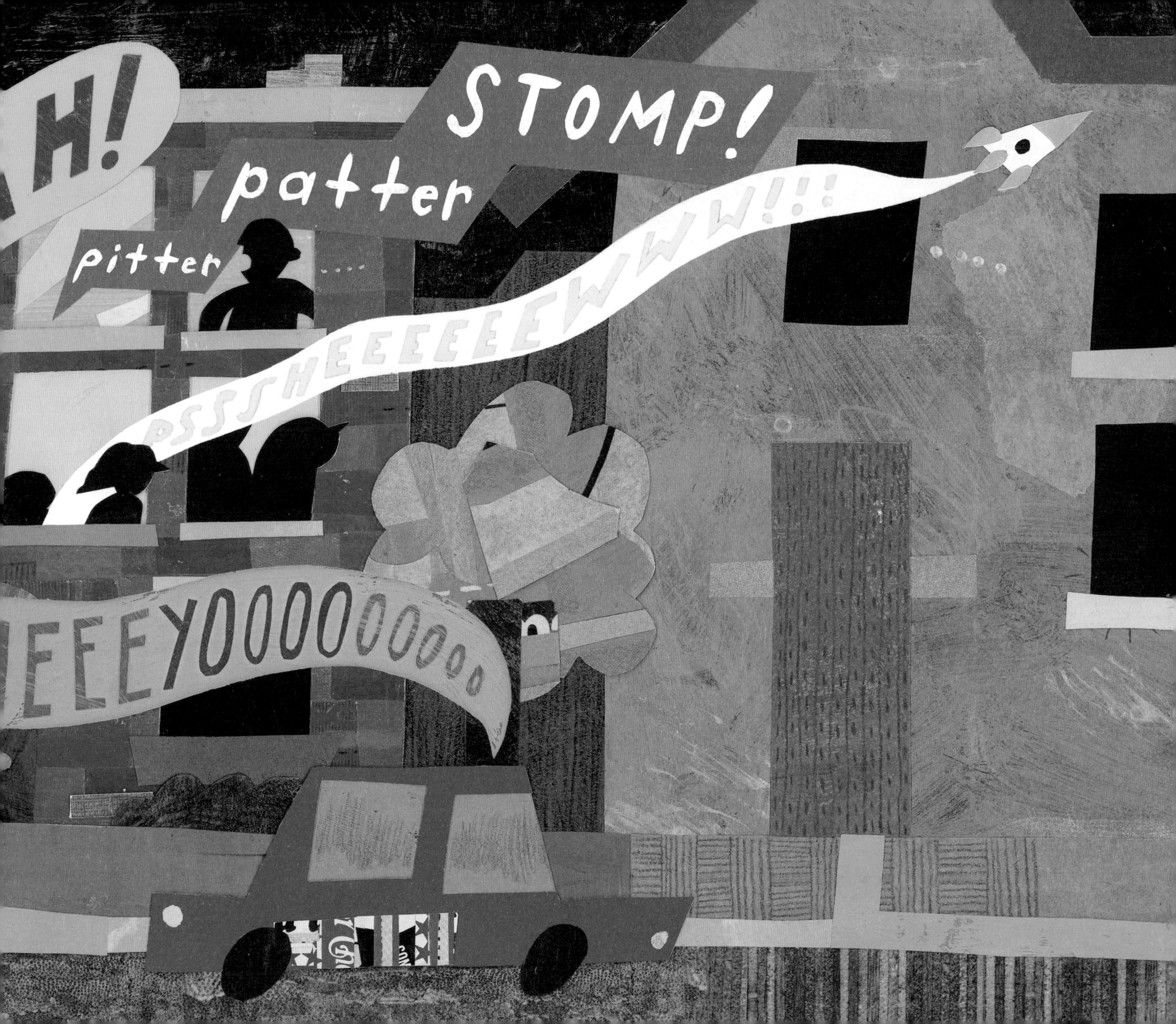
H!
STOMP!
patter
pitter
PSSSHEEEEEEEWWW!!!
EEEYOOOOOOOOO

Back on her perch,
Pepper curled up tight
and listened to the **shhhh shhhh**
of the street sweeper.

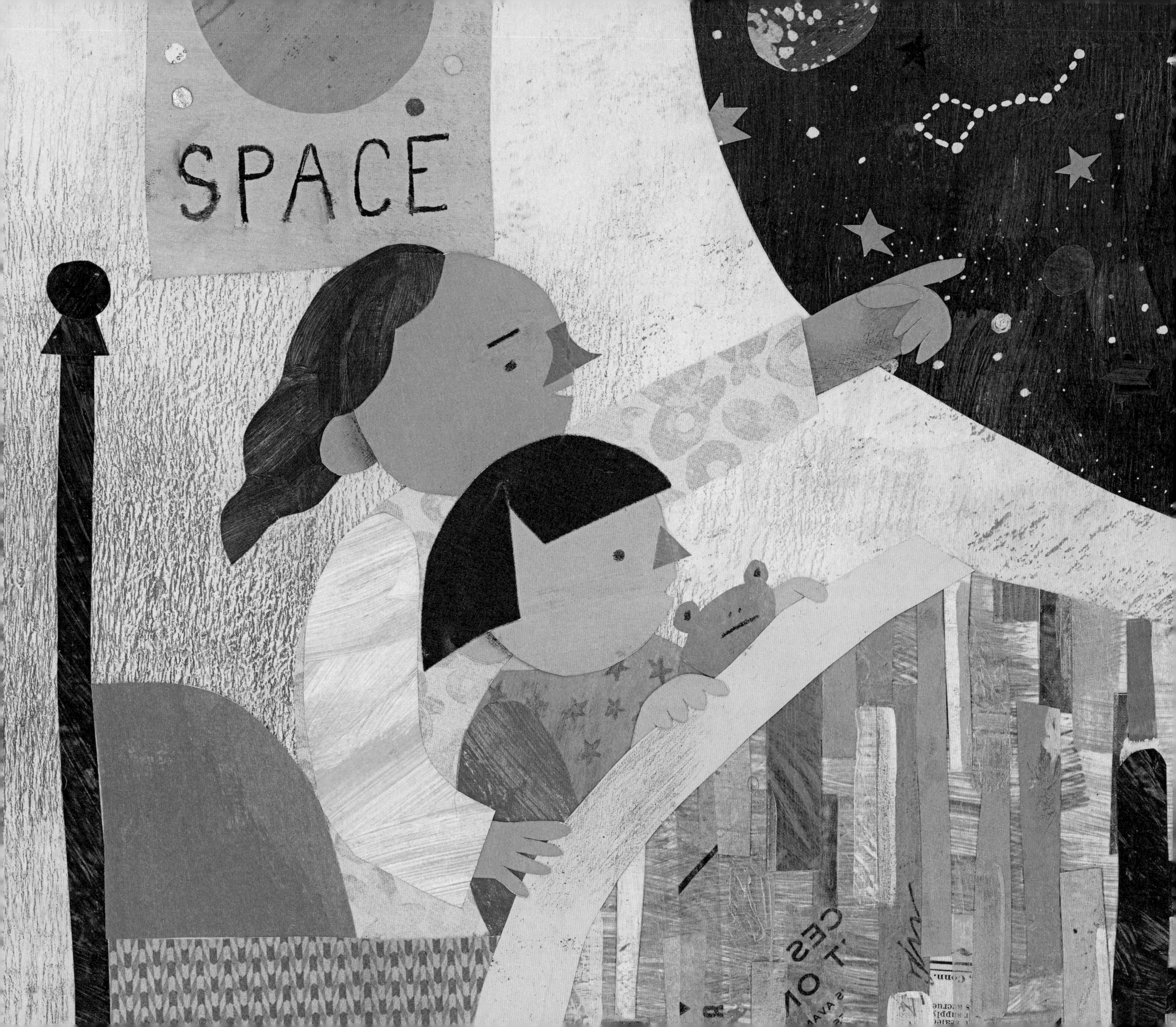
SPACE

Back in her bunk,
Natalia named the stars
and listened to the **shhhh shhhh**
and the **plonk plonk** of the falling acorns.

Back in their sleeping bags,
Cairo, Benny, and Miles closed their eyes
and listened to the **shhhh shhhh**,
the **plonk plonk**,
and the **ting ting** of the wind chime.

Back in his bed,

Rayhan burrowed under his covers

and listened to the **shhhh shhhh,**

the **plonk plonk,**

the **ting ting,**

and the **chhhp chhhp** of his parrot.

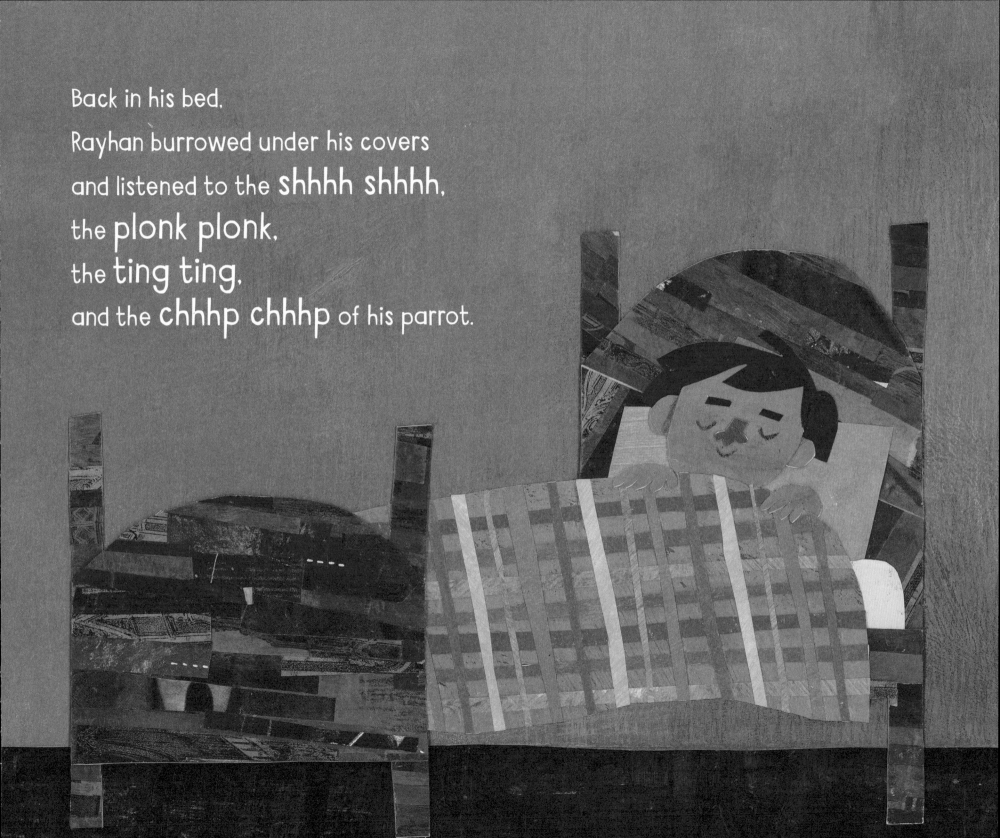

Back in her mother's arms,
Baby Izzie snuggled close
and listened to the **shhhh shhhh,**
the **plonk plonk,**
the **ting ting,**
the **chhhp chhhp,**
and the **pah-pum . . . pah-pum . . . pah-pum**
of her mother's heart.

Until . . .

everybody in the red brick building was asleep.